·A· CHRISTMAS· CAROL·

·A· CHRISTMAS · CAROL·

BEING A GHOST STORY OF CHRISTMAS

by Charles Dickens · abridged and illustrated by Mercer Mayer

Macmillan Publishing Company · New York

Collier Macmillan Publishers · London

A Paperwing Press Book. Abridgement and illustrations copyright © 1986 by Mercer Mayer. All rights reserved. No part of this book may be reproduced or transmitted in any form or by any means, electronic or mechanical, including photocopying, recording, or by any information storage and retrieval system, without permission in writing from the Publisher.

Macmillan Publishing Company, 866 Third Avenue, New York, NY 10022. Collier Macmillan Canada, Inc.

Printed and bound in Japan. First American Edition   10 9 8 7 6 5 4 3 2 1

Library of Congress Cataloging-in-Publication Data   Dickens, Charles, 1812–1870. A Christmas carol. Summary: An abridgment of the classic story with all the characters depicted as animals. [1. Christmas—Fiction. 2. Ghosts—Fiction. 3. England—Fiction. 4. Animals—Fiction] I. Mayer, Mercer, date, ill. II. Title. PZ7.D55Cg 1986 [Fic] 86-12651   ISBN 0-02-730310-1

In memory of
BILL   BACKER

Once upon a time—of all the good days in the year, on Christmas Eve—old Scrooge sat busy in his counting-house. It was cold, bleak, biting weather, and he could hear the people in the court outside go wheezing up and down, stamping their feet upon the pavement-stones to warm them. The city clocks had only just gone three, but it was quite dark already.

Scrooge kept a careful eye upon his clerk, who sat at a dismal little desk, copying letters. Scrooge had a very small fire, but the clerk's fire was so very much smaller that it looked like one coal.

Meanwhile, the fog and darkness thickened, and the cold became intense. Piercing, searching, biting cold. A boy outside bent down at Scrooge's keyhole and sang:

"God bless you merry gentlemen!
May nothing you dismay!"

"Bah! humbug!" said Scrooge.

At length, the hour of closing arrived, and Bob Cratchit, the clerk, instantly put on his scarf.

"You'll want all day to-morrow, I suppose?" said Scrooge.

"If quite convenient, Sir."

"It's not convenient," said Scrooge, "and it's not fair. I pay a day's wages for no work."

The clerk observed that it was only once a year.

"A poor excuse for picking a man's pockets every twenty-fifth of December!" said Scrooge, buttoning his great-coat to the chin. "But I suppose you must have the whole day. Be here all the earlier next morning."

The clerk promised that he would; and Scrooge walked out with a growl.

The office was closed in a twinkling. Scrooge took his melancholy dinner in his usual melancholy tavern. He read all the newspapers, and spent the rest of the evening with his banker's-book, and then went home to bed. He lived in chambers which had once belonged to his dead partner, Jacob Marley. They were a gloomy set of rooms in a great pile of a building up a yard. It was old and dreary, for nobody lived in it but Scrooge, the other rooms being let out as offices. The yard was so dark that even Scrooge, who knew its every stone, had to grope with his hands. The fog and frost hung about the black old gateway of the house.

Now, it is a fact, that there was nothing at all particular about the knob on the door, except that it was very large. It is also a fact, that Scrooge had seen it every night and morning since he had lived there. And it is also true that Scrooge had not given one thought to Marley since his partner's death seven years earlier. Then how did it happen that Scrooge, with his key in the lock of the door, saw not a knob, but Marley's face?

Marley's face. It had a dismal light about it. It was not angry or ferocious, but looked at Scrooge as Marley used to look.

As Scrooge gazed fixedly at it, it was a knob again.

To say that he was not startled would be untrue. But he put his hand upon the key, turned it sturdily, walked in, and lighted his candle. He *did* pause before he shut the door, and he *did* look cautiously behind it first. But there was nothing there, so he said "Pooh, pooh!" and closed it with a bang.

The sound resounded through the house like thunder. He fastened the door, and walked across the hall, and up the stairs. He walked through his rooms to see that all was right. Sitting-room, bed-room, lumber-room. All as they should be. Nobody under the table, nobody under the sofa, a small fire in the grate. Quite satisfied, he locked himself in; put on his dressing gown and slippers, and his night-cap; and sat down before the fire.

"Humbug!" said Scrooge.

As Scrooge sat there, he heard a clanking noise, deep down below, as if some person were dragging a heavy chain in the cellar. Scrooge then remembered that ghosts in haunted houses were described as dragging chains. The cellar-door flew open with a booming sound, and then he heard the noise much louder, on the floors below; then coming up the stairs; then coming straight towards his door.

"It's humbug still!" said Scrooge. "I won't believe it."

Without a pause, it came on through the heavy door, and passed into the room before his eyes. Upon its coming in, the dying flame leaped up, as though it cried "I know him! Marley's Ghost!" and fell again.

The chain the Ghost drew was clasped about his middle. It was made of ledgers, deeds, cash-boxes, keys, and padlocks wrought in steel. His body was transparent.

"Who are you?" asked Scrooge.

"In life I was your partner, Jacob Marley."

"Humbug, I tell you—humbug!" said Scrooge.

At this, the spirit raised a frightful cry, and shook its chain with such a dismal and appalling noise, that Scrooge held on tight to his chair.

"Mercy!" he said. "Dreadful apparition, why do you trouble me?"

"It is required of every man," the Ghost returned, "that the spirit within him should walk abroad among his fellow-men; and if that spirit goes not forth in life, it is condemned to do so after death. It is doomed to wander through the world, and witness what it cannot share, but might have shared on earth, and turned to happiness!

"I wear the chain I forged in life," said the Ghost. "My spirit never walked beyond our counting house. Hear me!" cried the Ghost. "My time is nearly gone. I am here to-night to warn you, that you have yet a chance of escaping my fate. You will be haunted by Three Spirits. Expect the first to-morrow, when the bell tolls one. Expect the second on the next night at the same hour. The third upon the next night when the last stroke of twelve has ceased to vibrate. Look to see me no more; and look that, for your own sake, you remember what has passed between us!"

Scrooge tried to say "Humbug!" but stopped at the first syllable. He went straight to bed, and fell asleep immediately.

When he awoke, it was very dark. Suddenly he remembered that the Ghost had warned him of a visitation when the bell tolled one. The bell sounded, with a deep, dull, hollow ONE. Light flashed in the room, and the curtains of his bed were drawn aside. Scrooge found himself face to face with an unearthly visitor. It wore a tunic of the purest white, and a lustrous belt, and the dress was trimmed with summer flowers.

"Are you the Spirit whose coming was foretold to me?" asked Scrooge.

"I am the Ghost of Christmas Past."

"Long past?" inquired Scrooge.

"No. Your past."

The Spirit put out a hand as it spoke, and clasped him gently by the arm.

"Rise! and walk with me!"

As the words were spoken, they passed through the wall, and stood upon an open country road, with fields on either hand. The city had entirely vanished.

"Good heaven!" said Scrooge, clasping his hands together, as he looked about him. "I was bred in this place. I was a boy here!"

They walked along the road; Scrooge recognising every gate, and post, and tree; until a little market-town appeared in the distance.

They came to a school.

"It is not quite deserted," said the Ghost. "A solitary child, neglected by his friends, is left there still."

Scrooge said he knew it. And he sobbed.

Now they were in the busy thoroughfares of a city. It was evening, and the streets were lighted up. Here too it was Christmas time again.

The Ghost stopped at a certain warehouse door, and asked Scrooge if he knew it.

"Know it!" said Scrooge. "Was I apprenticed here?"

They went in. At the sight of an old gentleman sitting behind a high desk, Scrooge cried in great excitement:

"Why, it's old Fezziwig! Bless his heart, it's Fezziwig alive again!"

Old Fezziwig laid down his pen, and looked up at the clock.

"Yo ho, there! Ebenezer! Dick!"

Scrooge's former self, now a young man, came briskly in, accompanied by a fellow apprentice.

"Yo ho, my boys!" said Fezziwig. "No more work to-night. Christmas Eve, Dick. Christmas, Ebenezer!"

Again, Scrooge and the Ghost stood side by side in the open air.

"My time grows short," observed the spirit. "Quick!"

This was not addressed to Scrooge, or to any one whom he could see, but it produced an immediate effect. For again Scrooge saw himself. He was older now; a man in the prime of life. His face had not the harsh and rigid lines of later years; but it had begun to wear the signs of care and avarice. There was an eager, greedy, restless motion in the eye.

He was not alone, but sat by the side of a fair young girl, in whose eyes there were tears.

"It matters little," she said softly. "To you, very little. Another idol has displaced me."

"What Idol has displaced you?" he asked.

"A golden one. Gain engrosses you."

"Spirit!" said Scrooge in a broken voice, "remove me from this place."

"I told you these were shadows of the things that have been," said the Ghost. "That they are what they are, do not blame me!"

"Remove me!" Scrooge exclaimed. "I cannot bear it! Take me back. Haunt me no longer!"

Scrooge was conscious of being exhausted, and overcome by drowsiness; and, further, of being in his own bedroom. He had barely time to reel to bed, before he sank into a heavy sleep. He awakened in the middle of a great snore, and sat up in bed to get his thoughts together. He knew that the bell was about to strike one, and felt that he had awakened in the nick of time. He turned uncomfortably cold when he began to wonder which of his curtains the new Spirit would draw back, so he established a sharp look-out for it. When the Bell struck One, and no shape appeared, he was taken with a violent fit of trembling. Five minutes, ten minutes, a quarter of an hour went by, yet nothing came. As he watched, he saw a blaze of ruddy light, which was more alarming than a dozen ghosts. He began to think that the source and secret of this light might be in the adjoining room, from whence it seemed to shine. He got up softly and shuffled in his slippers to the door.

The moment Scrooge's hand was on the lock, a strange voice called him by his name, and bade him enter. He obeyed.

It was his own room. There was no doubt about that. Heaped upon the floor, to form a kind of throne, were turkeys, geese, game, poultry, great joints of meat, long wreaths of sausages, mince-pies, plum-puddings, barrels of oysters, red-hot chestnuts, cherry-cheeked apples, juicy oranges, luscious pears, and seething bowls of punch. Above it sat a jolly Giant, glorious to see.

"I am the Ghost of Christmas Present," said the Spirit. "Look upon me!"

Scrooge reverently did so. It was clothed in a simple robe, bordered with white fur. On its head it wore a holly wreath.

"You have never seen the like of me before!" exclaimed the Spirit.

"Never," Scrooge said. "Spirit, conduct me where you will."

"Touch my robe!" said the Spirit.

Scrooge did as he was told, and held it fast.

Holly, turkeys, geese, game, poultry, meat, sausages, oysters, pies, puddings, fruit, and punch, all vanished instantly. So did the room, the fire, the ruddy glow, the hour of night, and they stood in the city streets on Christmas morning. Many of the shops were still half open, radiant in their glory. But soon the steeples called good people all, to church and chapel, and away they came. At the same time there emerged from streets and lanes people carrying their dinners to the bakers' shops to be cooked. And near the docks, there were many poor creatures who had nothing at all, but who stood in line with their tin plates, waiting for whatever was doled out to them.

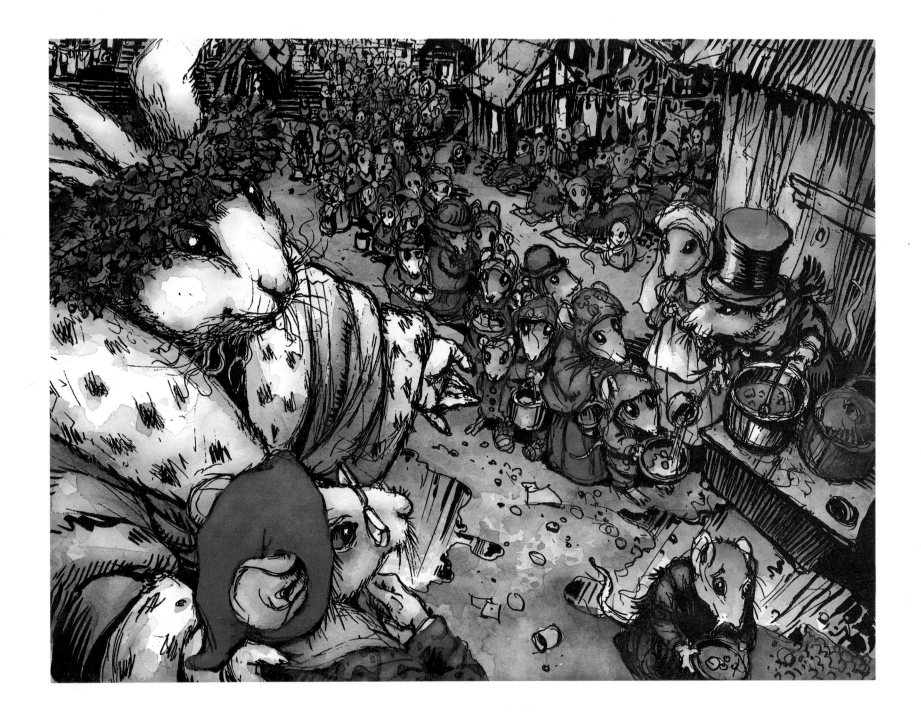

Scrooge watched them, and then they went on, invisible, as they had been before, into the suburbs of the town. It was a remarkable quality of the Ghost that despite his size, he could fit himself into any place with ease, and could stand beneath a low roof quite as gracefully as he could have done in any lofty hall. And it was perhaps the pleasure the good Spirit had in showing off this power of his, or else his sympathy with all poor men, that led him straight to Scrooge's clerk's. For there he went, and took Scrooge with him, holding to his robe; and on the threshold of the door the Spirit smiled, and stopped to bless Bob Cratchit's dwelling.

Such a bustle went on inside as the family prepared their Christmas dinner. Bob took Tiny Tim beside him, leaning on his crutch, and the young Cratchits set chairs for everybody. At last the dishes were set on, and grace was said. As the goose was served, Tiny Tim beat on the table with the handle of his knife and cried Hurrah!

At last the dinner was all done. At Bob Cratchit's elbow stood the family display of glass; four tumblers, and a custard-cup without a handle. Bob poured the Christmas punch into them, and proposed:

"A Merry Christmas to us all, my dears. God bless us!"

Which all the family re-echoed.

"God bless us every one!" said Tiny Tim, the last of all.

He sat very close to his father's side, upon his little stool. Bob held his withered little hand in his, as if he loved the child, and wished to keep him by his side, and dreaded that he might be taken from him.

"Spirit," said Scrooge, with an interest he had never felt before, "tell me if Tiny Tim will live."

"I see a vacant seat," replied the Ghost, "in the poor chimney corner, and a crutch without an owner, carefully preserved. If these shadows remain unaltered by the Future, the child will die."

The bell struck twelve.

Scrooge looked about him for the Ghost, and saw it not. As the last stroke ceased to vibrate, he remembered the prediction of old Jacob Marley. Lifting up his eyes, he beheld a solemn Phantom, draped and hooded, coming towards him. It was shrouded in a deep black garment, which concealed its form, and left nothing visible save one outstretched hand. Its mysterious presence filled him with a solemn dread.

"I am in the presence of the Ghost of Christmas Yet To Come?" said Scrooge.

The spirit answered not, but pointed downward with its hand.

"You are about to show me shadows of the things that have not happened, but will happen in the time before us," Scrooge pursued. "Is that so, Spirit?"

Although well used to ghostly company by this time, Scrooge feared the silent shape so much that his legs trembled beneath him, and he found that he could hardly stand when he prepared to follow it.

"Lead on!" said Scrooge. "Lead on! The night is waning fast, and it is precious time to me, I know. Lead on, Spirit!"

The Phantom moved away as it had come towards him. Scrooge followed in the shadow of its dress. The Phantom glided on into a street. Scrooge accompanied it until they reached an iron gate. He paused to look round before entering.

A churchyard. Here, then, the wretched man whose name he had now to learn, lay underneath the ground. It was a worthy place. Walled in by houses; overrun by grass and weeds, the growth of vegetation's death, not life.

The Spirit stood among the graves, and pointed down to One. He advanced towards it trembling. The Phantom was exactly as it had been, but he dreaded that he saw new meaning in its solemn shape. Scrooge crept towards it, trembling as he went; and following the finger, read upon the stone of the neglected grave his own name, EBENEZER SCROOGE.

The finger pointed from the grave to him, and back again.

"No, Spirit! Oh no, no!"

The finger still was there.

"Spirit!" he cried, tight clutching at its robe, "hear me! I am not the man I was. I will not be the man I must have been. Good Spirit, assure me that I yet may change these shadows you have shown me, by an altered life!"

The kind hand trembled.

"I will honor Christmas in my heart, and try to keep it all the year. I will live in the Past, the Present, and the Future. The Spirits of all Three shall strive within me. I will not shut out the lessons that they teach. Oh, tell me I may sponge away the writing on this stone!"

Holding up his hands in one last prayer to have his fate reversed, he saw an alteration in the Phantom's hood and dress. It shrunk, collapsed, and dwindled down into a bedpost.

Yes! And the bedpost was his own. The bed was his own, the room was his own. Best and happiest of all, the Time before him was his own, to make amends in!

"I will live in the Past, the Present, and the Future!" Scrooge repeated, as he scrambled out of bed. "The Spirits of all Three shall strive within me. Oh Jacob Marley! Heaven, and the Christmas Time be praised for this! I say it on my knees, old Jacob; on my knees!"

He was so fluttered and so glowing with his good intentions, that his broken voice would scarcely answer to his call. He had been sobbing violently in his conflict with the Spirit, and his face was wet with tears.

"I don't know what to do!" cried Scrooge, laughing and crying in the same breath. "I don't know what day of the month it is!" said Scrooge. "I don't know how long I've been among the Spirits. I don't know anything!"

Running to the window, he opened it, and put out his head. No fog, no mist; clear, bright, jovial, stirring, cold; cold, piping for the blood to dance to; Golden sunlight, Heavenly sky; sweet fresh air; merry bells. Oh, glorious. Glorious!

"What's to-day?" cried Scrooge, calling downward to a boy in Sunday clothes.

"To-day!" replied the boy. "Why, CHRISTMAS DAY."

"Hallo, my fine fellow! Do you know the Poulterer's, in the next street but one?" Scrooge inquired. "Do you know whether they've sold the prize Turkey that was hanging up there?"

"What, the one as big as me?" returned the boy.

"What a delightful boy!" said Scrooge. "It's a pleasure to talk to him. Yes, my buck!"

"It's hanging there now," replied the boy.

"Go and buy it," said Scrooge, "and tell 'em to bring it here."

The boy was off like a shot.

"I'll send it to Bob Cratchit's!" whispered Scrooge, splitting with a laugh. "He sha'n't know who sends it. It's twice the size of Tiny Tim."

He dressed himself "all in his best," and at last got out into the streets. The people were by this time pouring forth; and walking with his hands behind him, Scrooge regarded every one with a delighted smile. He went to church, and walked about the streets, and watched the people, and patted children on the head, and questioned beggars, and found that everything could yield him pleasure.

The next morning, he was early at the office. "A merry Christmas, Bob!" said Scrooge. "A merrier Christmas, Bob, my good fellow, than I have given you, for many a year! I'll raise your salary, and endeavour to assist your struggling family, and we will discuss your affairs this very afternoon, over a Christmas bowl of smoking bishop, Bob!"

Scrooge was better than his word. He did it all, and infinitely more; and to Tiny Tim, who did NOT die, he was a second father. He became as good a friend, as good a master, and as good a man, as the good old city knew. And it was always said of him, that he knew how to keep Christmas well, if any man alive possessed the knowledge. May that be truly said of us, and all of us! And so, as Tiny Tim observed, God Bless Us, Every One!

Mercer Mayer prepared the artwork for this book
in pen-and-ink and watercolor
on Strathmore watercolor paper.
The text has been set in 14 point Sabon
by Vulcan Typography Company,
with display in Caslon Antique.
The separations, printing, and binding were done
by Toppan Printing Co. (America) Inc., in Tokyo.